Walt Disney's Mickey and Friends

# Haunted Halloween

*By Diane Muldrow*

*Illustrated by Scott Tilley and Brent Ford*

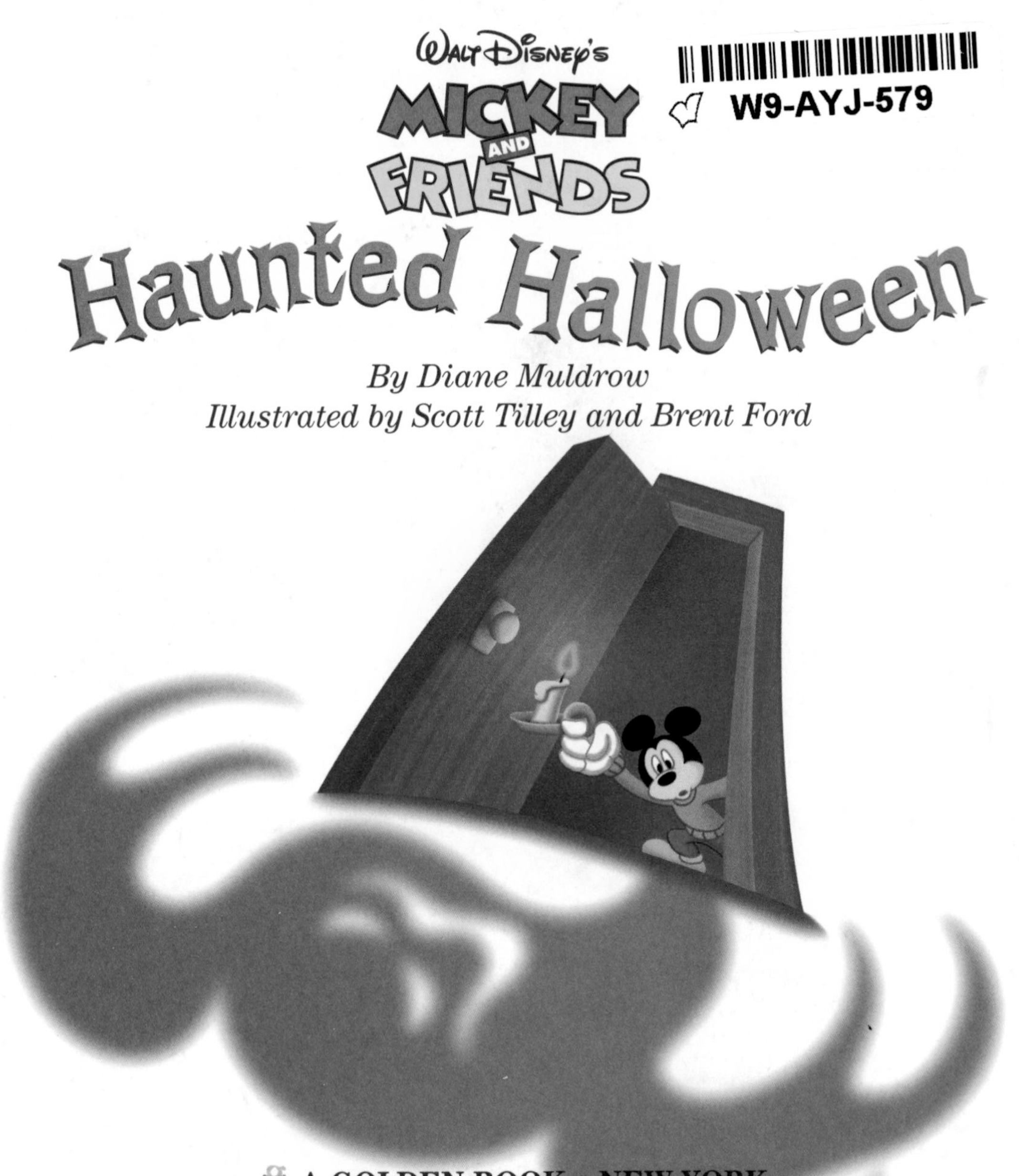



A GOLDEN BOOK • NEW YORK

Golden Books Publishing Company, Inc., New York, New York 10106


Library of Congress Catalog Card Number: 97-80828 ISBN: 0-307-96006-4 A MCMXCVIII First Edition 1998

"I am going to have a terrific Halloween party tonight," Mickey said to himself. "If I ever finish getting ready!"

Mickey tacked one last fake cobweb to the wall. "Now it's time to make the popcorn balls," he said.

An hour later, Mickey looked around his spooky living room. "Everything looks great!" he said happily.

Mickey glanced at the clock. "Golly!" he added. "It's almost time for the party, and I haven't put my costume together yet!"

Mickey knew he had an old pirate costume tucked away somewhere in the attic.

Up, up a creaky ladder he headed, into the dark attic.
"Now, just where did I put that costume?" Mickey wondered. As soon as he switched on the light, thunder crashed outdoors.

Lightning flashed across the sky. Then out went the attic light!

"Oh, dear!" Mickey said as he stumbled around in the dark. Just then he blundered into a huge cobweb.

"Yikes!" he said with a shudder. "These spiderwebs are all over the place!"

Luckily, the light quickly came back on again.

"Thank goodness," Mickey said. "Ah-aah-choo! There's an awful lot of dust up here!"

Finally, Mickey found the old trunk he'd been looking for.

"Aachoo!" Mickey sneezed again. "I'll bet my pirate costume's in here.

Mickey turned the key in the rusty old lock and got the trunk open.

"AAAGHH!" Mickey shouted. A skeleton grinned up at him! Then Mickey realized that it was just a plastic party decoration. "Whew!" he said in relief. "What a good Halloween joke on me! This skeleton will be perfect for my party!"

"I'd better take the whole trunk downstairs," Mickey thought to himself as he rummaged through it. "There's a lot of cool Halloween stuff in here!"

Meanwhile, in Mickey's backyard, Pluto had been chasing a ball through the sheets hanging on the clothesline.

As Pluto charged under one sheet, it came loose from the line and fell on top of him. It covered him from head to tail.

Suddenly, rain began to fall. The wet sheet stuck to Pluto like glue. No matter how hard he tried, he couldn't shake it off. And he couldn't see anything, either!

It really began to pour as Donald, Goofy, Minnie, and Daisy drove up to Mickey's house.

"Gawrsh! Look at the lightning!" Goofy exclaimed.

"It's a spooky Halloween night," said Daisy with a nervous giggle.

"Let's run right into the house," said Minnie. "If we wait for Mickey to answer the door, our costumes will get soaked."

*BOOM!* went the thunder as Mickey's friends hurried into his house.

"Mickey, we're here!" called Minnie. "Where are you?"

But Mickey didn't answer. He was still in the attic, too far upstairs to hear anything over the sounds of the storm.

Just then, the lights went out again! "Uh-oh!" said Donald.

*THUMP—KA-THUMP—THUMP!* The bumping sounds were coming from somewhere above.

"Wh-what was that?" Minnie gasped.

Then they heard something big and heavy being slowly dragged across the floor upstairs!

"It-it sounds like a coffin being dragged across Mickey's room!" whispered Goofy.

Meanwhile, in the backyard, poor Pluto was still stuck under the sheet. He couldn't see to find his doggie door.

"Aaaarrr! Arr! Arr!" Pluto howled.

"What's that sound?" Donald whispered to his friends.

"Ssshhh!" Minnie whispered back.

Just then, something weird and white ran past the window.

"It's a g-g-ghost!" exclaimed Daisy.

Mickey's friends were too scared even to scream!

Meanwhile, upstairs, Mickey lit a candle and changed into his costume.

Then, picking up the skeleton decoration, he slowly and carefully headed down the dark staircase.

Mickey's friends heard a slow shuffling of feet and a rattling of bones. They looked up to see a horrible monster coming toward them. This time, everybody screamed!

Suddenly, the lights came back on.

“Hi, everybody,” Mickey said in surprise. “You really scared me!”

“Oh, Mickey! It’s just you!” cried Minnie. “You really scared us!”

"I love your scary costume," said Donald with a shiver.

Daisy picked up a cupcake and began to munch. "Mickey," she said, "this is the scariest, most exciting Halloween ever! How did you do it?"

"Gawrsh, Mickey, it's the best haunted house I've ever been in," added Goofy.

"Er—haunted house?" said a puzzled Mickey, looking around.

Just then, Pluto finally found his way in through the doggie door. He happily galloped into the living room.

It was the ghost! Mickey and his friends screamed!

"Arf!" barked Pluto.

"Oh, Pluto! It's you!" said Mickey in relief. "Hey, boy, you're all wet! Let's get you dried off!"

“You’re right,” Mickey told his friends with a laugh, as he dried Pluto with a towel. “This *is* the scariest Halloween ever!”